Pray with your G.A..!
Arlene Hebert

Endorsements

"Young readers will be swept up in the rigors of a saga through boot camp for angels. Meet Anjo and Angelle, a duo of fresh faced recruits with a very special mission. Arlene Hebert's rich text moves us from hallowed halls of learning, past troubled earthy playgrounds, on to flower filled meadows in the clouds. It's not all serenity as the two young guardian angels float, bump and jolt their way through a program grooming them to be the personal guardians of a set of twins, yet to be born. Every resource of God's Kingdom is made available to the two young heroes as they make ready to stand and fight for precious new charges."

- Frank Remkiewicz

Children's Book Author & Illustrator

"Arlene Hebert's Angeltales is one of the most delightful series of books for young children to come out in a very long time. She presents the stories winsomely, in language both children and adults can visualize and enjoy. Where many books about God show Him to be thunderous and fierce, Mrs. Hebert's stories show Him as a loving Father, patient and kind, and with a great sense of humor. The little angels, Angelle and Anjo, have characteristics with which children will identify, and the twin babies they 'look after' are realistically portrayed as energetic, curious little ones. I wholeheartedly endorse these volumes."

- Shirley Comeaux, Ph.D.

Educator and Reading Specialist

This Book Belongs to...

name

Thank you for purchasing book three of the
Angeltale Adventure Series. I know that you'll
have fun traveling on adventures with
Angelle and Anjo as they go their separate
ways with Celeste and Michael. Enjoy the story
and God Bless!

Arlene Hebert

To Purchase Books and Products

Visit the new and exciting website for children, **www.angeltaleadventures.com**, where copies of all books and release dates of upcoming Angeltale Adventures are available in the Angeltale Book Store.

Limited Edition prints of the artwork featured throughout this book and others are available for purchase in the Book Store as well. All prints are available in black and white with selected prints in color. These frame-ready prints, signed and numbered by the artist, can be hung in classrooms, children's rooms or collected by children of all ages.

The Angel Brigade Club

A Note From the Author

If we as adults believe that the future of the world belongs to the children of today, then we MUST help teach children NOW how to make better choices.

The Angel Brigade Club was created for that purpose. The club will help unite children and encourage them to make better choices in their lives. Through one good decision at a time, children can change the future of the world.

This club teaches children that angels are real; they are all around us. As Christians, we believe that there is that special angel entrusted to assist and guide each one of us through life. These invisible servants of God are standing ready to help; we just have to call on them. ANGEL POWER ACTIVATE!

Visit **www.angeltaleadventures.com** to enroll in the club. Children are encouraged to name their guardian angels, sign the Book of Life (featured in book two of the series), take the pledge – Take Back Our World – and print the frame-ready certificate, print the FREE quarterly newsletters and purchase the club T-shirt. The Angel Brigade Club Quarterly Newsletter NO. 1 has ideas for newly-forming clubs. Unique club ideas can be shared by e-mailing me through the site. Your idea could be featured in future newsletters.

Please help me make this a wonderful opportunity for our children and grandchildren.

Angels in Training: Promised Adventures

Angels in Training: Promised Adventures

Written by
Arlene B. Hebert

Illustrated by
Peter Berchman DeHart

Book Three

The Angeltale Adventures

Miss Doll Publishing
A Division of Miss Doll, Inc.

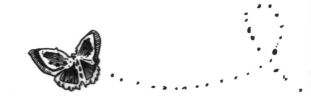

The Angeltale Adventures

Library of Congress Cataloging in Publication Data
ISBN 13: 9780981926421

Published by Miss Doll Publishing
A division of Miss Doll, Inc.
P. O. Box 63034
Lafayette, Louisiana 70596-3034

Illustrated by Peter DeHart
Design and layout by Peter DeHart
Edited by Shirley Comeaux, Ph.D., Nancy Burns, Joyce Michel, Michelle Truxillo and Sonja Davis
Printed in the United States of America

Dedication

To my husband of thirty-six years, Lyon;
your love and support has allowed me to
experience the adventure as a children's
author. I love you.

To my two daughters, Ashley and Lindsey;
my son-in-law, Tim; and my grandson,
Gunner; I count my blessings often when
I think of each one of you. I love you
all.

Contents

The Adventure Continues   1

CHAPTER ONE   3
Angelle and Anjo
Meet Celeste and Michael

CHAPTER TWO   7
Angelle and Celeste
Visit the Valley of Peace

CHAPTER THREE   12
Anjo Spends Time with Michael

CHAPTER FOUR   17
Anjo's Lessons Continue

CHAPTER FIVE   21
Celeste Shares Dreams with Angelle

CHAPTER SIX   26
Anjo and Michael
Visit the Kingdom of Lost Souls

CHAPTER SEVEN   30
Anjo and Michael Visit Earth

CHAPTER EIGHT   36
True Beauty is on the Inside

CHAPTER NINE   44
Graduation Day Has Arrived

Let's Talk About . . .   49

About the Author   53

About the Illustrator   55

Other Angeltale Books   56

Angels in Training

Promised Adventures

THE ADVENTURE CONTINUES

Twin Angel School was officially over for Angelle and Anjo. They were the chosen team of guardian angels for Sarah and Matthew, the special twins God would soon create. All the angels in Heaven could hardly wait for this big event.

It wasn't every day that God decided to create children who could see and talk with their guardian angels, but that was God's exact plan. God had an important reason for making this happen; He was concerned about His people on Earth.

God wanted to re-teach valuable lessons that were ignored and long forgotten in the world. The twins would learn these lessons through the interaction and friendship with their angels. They would then pass the lessons on to other children. Through this network of children, the behavior and actions of many would change.

God would save the world through the children. It was an awesome plan, one that would succeed over time. The story goes like this...

ANGELLE AND ANJO MEET CELESTE AND MICHAEL

The formal training for Angelle and Anjo was now over. Their little angel-brains were saturated with valuable knowledge. As a reward for their hard work in school, God arranged a big surprise for each of them.

Anjo only dreamed about his travels with Michael, but today in Heaven, God ordered it to happen. Michael the Archangel and Celeste, the

Angel of Love and Beauty, approached God. Anjo hardly noticed the interesting angel by Michael's side; Angelle, on the other hand, stared at Celeste.

Celeste and Michael knelt before God and bowed their heads. God passed His hand over them as He blessed them. Before Michael could stand and greet his new partner, Anjo was hovering before him face-to-face. God and Michael chuckled.

Michael stood slowly and said, "Hello, Anjo, I've looked forward to our meeting. I'm glad Father is allowing us to spend time together."

Anjo was now speechless looking Michael up and down. He seemed taller than Cloud Mountain, Anjo thought. Angel-bumps surfaced on Anjo's arms and legs as excitement traveled through his spirit body.

"Will I need a shield and a sword, Michael?"

"Not just yet, Anjo." Michael turned his back towards him. "Grab hold," he commanded. "We must be off; Lucifer never ceases with his evil ways. Hold on tight." Anjo grabbed hold to Michael's wings. In seconds, they were out of sight.

Even though Angelle was excited to spend time with Celeste, sadness pierced her heart at the thought of leaving God's Presence. God looked into her big green eyes and knew of her heartache. He bent slightly towards her to receive her sweet kiss on His cheek. Then God gently turned her toward Celeste, and together they soared off to a planned destination.

Through their adventures, Angelle and Anjo would learn what the school motto meant: angels never stop learning valuable lessons. Yes, their angel-wisdom would only increase over time.

ANGELLE AND CELESTE
VISIT THE VALLEY OF PEACE

Celeste and Angelle arrived in a valley of rolling hills and meadows. Pink, red, yellow, orange and purple flowers were everywhere.

"How beautiful!" Angelle said.

"It is lovely," Celeste said as her eyes roamed the area. "I'm still amazed at the beauty God created for us. Welcome to the Valley of Peace."

Angelle closed her eyes and took a deep

breath. "What's that smell?"

"It's called springtime – a mixture of rose, gardenia and honeysuckle," Celeste said.

They floated through the valley. Angelle's eyes danced from one scene to another: a waterfall of light blue, crystal water; a pasture of orange and purple poppies; and a mountain of green and yellow gemstones. Beautiful scenes were in every direction.

"I can see why this place is called the Valley of Peace. What do angels do here?" Angelle asked.

"Angels come here after completing their missions. They rest in Father's peace while they get ready for their next assignments. When I came here, I learned to become a storyteller so that I could help little angels like you," she said. "So let's start with my favorite story, the creation of Heaven and the angels."

Together they settled in a large patch of pink and red clover on the top of a hill. Celeste's first story was about Lucifer – the Angel of Light, one of the most beautiful angels ever created by God. "The first thing you need to understand is that God gives all angels a will of their own, just like He gives mankind. It's their choice to serve God."

"What angel would not want to serve God?" asked Angelle.

"Well, Lucifer decided just that. He was full of pride," Celeste said. "He knew he was beautiful, but he wasn't satisfied. He wanted to be equal to God. Imagine that!"

"Lucifer might have been a beautiful angel, but he wasn't too smart," Angelle said. "It's impossible for any angel to be like God."

"Precisely!" Celeste said. "In addition to Lucifer's bad choice, other angels chose to follow him."

Angelle was shocked. She couldn't believe what she was hearing. "I learned in school that all choices have consequences. What happened?"

"God threw Lucifer and his followers out of the Kingdom of Heaven for all eternity," Celeste said. "He now roams Earth with his evil angels creating turmoil in the world. His mission is to cause human beings to lose their souls forever.

"The world has developed many names and stories about him," she continued. "They call him Satan, the Devil, the Dragon; any ugly name fits him. I don't even like talking about him or saying his name. I refer to him as the Evil One; that's good enough for me."

Celeste spent much time explaining how evil has spread all over the world and Angelle paid close attention to every detail.

"You and Anjo must teach Sarah and Matthew how to recognize Satan's evil work. God will use these children in a very special way," Celeste emphasized. "They will be God's champions for good; His instruments of change. Yes, God will use Sarah and Matthew in a mighty way."

ANJO SPENDS TIME
WITH MICHAEL

Michael and Anjo traveled through the heavens to the Warring Angel Headquarters. This territory was so huge from the air that Anjo could hardly believe his eyes.

Their landing was smooth, quite the opposite from Anjo's own landings. Anjo realized he had much more to learn about using his new wings. He intended to talk with Michael about his flying, when in an instant, he found himself in the midst of gazillions of large, muscular angels preparing for battle. Anjo was speechless!

"This is God's heavenly army under my command," Michael said. "He instructs me and I do His Will. Lucifer and the other fallen angels continue to create evil in the world where humans live. Our mission is to fight his army and save souls."

"Michael, your job is so important. I'd like to be an archangel like you one day."

When Anjo said those words, he knew he'd said the wrong thing. He could feel it inside, and it didn't make him feel good. He took a deep breath and lowered his head.

"Oh, Michael, Father will be so disappointed in me if He heard my words."

"He did hear your words, Anjo."

Anjo's eyes shot upward and met Michael's. "He did?" Anjo asked.

"Father hears and knows all things," Michael explained. "That's one of His reasons for allowing you to spend time with me."

"I don't understand," Anjo said.

"We have much to talk about. There's no better time than now."

Michael searched for an area secluded from all the activity in the Warring Center. He sat on a large boulder and pulled Anjo onto his knee.

"Anjo, you need to be the angel that God created you to be. God had good reasons for making you a guardian angel. You don't want to be an archangel like me."

Michael paused for a moment and thought. "You see, Anjo, that's a big problem on Earth. Human beings do the same thing. They spend so much time, energy and money trying to be like someone else. Deep inside, those people are not happy.

"God gave each person unique gifts. When they try to be like someone else, they don't use their gifts and talents. It's like saying 'no, thank You, God, for making me special.' And I know you don't want to do that to Father."

"Michael, I love Father so much. I never want to hurt Him like that. It just seems like being an archangel is real cool," Anjo said.

"Doing God's Will is what's cool," Michael stressed. "His Will is for you to be the best guardian angel you can be."

Anjo thought for a while. He began to

understand how unique he was and how
important it was to be himself.

"You're right, Michael. I don't want to
disappoint Father again. I want Him to be
proud of me."

"He will," Michael said. "I promise."

ANJO'S LESSONS CONTINUE

Anjo had just learned his first lesson with Michael. Be the angel God created him to be echoed in his head. Michael's mission though, was to show him much more. As they prepared to leave, Michael gave orders to the leading war angels. Armored with large, copper- and pewter-colored metal suits, swords and shields, angels departed in different directions.

"Michael, why doesn't God just wipe out

Lucifer's army? I know He can do it with only a command," Anjo said.

"Every day millions of people on Earth ask that same question. God's plan is a great mystery to all," Michael said. "What you must remember is that God's glory will shine above all evil on the last day. He will destroy Lucifer and his army. And I will throw Lucifer into the deepest and darkest hole for the rest of eternity."

"Michael, being the leader of God's royal army is an awesome job."

"Anjo, you can help me and the warring angels fight evil by helping Matthew. When you guide Matthew to choose good instead of evil, you help defeat Lucifer's bad angels. That's also the mission of guardian angels," Michael said.

"Gee! I never thought of that," Anjo said. "I really am part of God's army."

"Yes, you are," Michael said. "We work together."

Anjo seemed to grow in size as he thought

about being part of the heavenly army. He could now see how guardian angels and warring angels make up God's heavenly army.

This new knowledge made Anjo want to be the best G.A.(Guardian Angel) under God. He was finally content in being who God created him to be: HIMSELF.

CELESTE SHARES DREAMS WITH ANGELLE

Celeste spent much time teaching Angelle about Lucifer and the ways of the evil ones. To change the subject, she rolled down the hill and Angelle followed. They settled in another patch of white-puffed flowers that smelled like popcorn and looked like snow. They laid in the flowers and made angel imprints in them. While Celeste told one story after another with great enthusiasm, a

golden butterfly appeared and circled them. Celeste held out her hand, and the butterfly landed on her finger.

"Hello, Beauty," Celeste said, "meet Angelle." The butterfly flitted over to Angelle and settled fearlessly on her finger.

"Do you talk with butterflies a lot?" Angelle asked.

"Yes. This is my favorite spot. I love to sit

here, visit with my little friends, watch the clouds and dream. The other angels call me Dream Angel," she said with a chuckle. "When I'm not talking to little angels like you, I'm making up dreams for Father to give little children when they sleep."

"That's neat," Angelle said with interest. "What kind of dreams do you make up?"

"All kinds of wonderful dreams," Celeste said. "God is about everything that is good and fun. He never sends children bad dreams; only beautiful dreams like He is."

"Tell me one," Angelle encouraged.

"OK," Celeste paused to think. "Once, there was a little girl who lost her grandmother to cancer, a dreadful disease. The little girl cried often because she loved and missed her grandmother. So God directed me to send the child a dream letting her know that her grandmother was all right."

"What was the dream about?" Angelle asked.

"In the dream the little girl spotted her

grandmother standing in the front of a big church. The grandmother turned around and smiled at her granddaughter. The love that exchanged between the two of them was fulfilling for the child. Her grandmother looked wonderful to her.

"I sent that same dream to the little girl on many different nights. Over time, she realized that wherever her grandmother was, she was no longer suffering and sick, but happy and well. The child then experienced peace."

"Wow, Father loves and cares about His children on Earth so much," Angelle said. "Tell me another story."

"OK," Celeste said. "Dream number two, just for you.

"Once, there was a little boy who was lonesome after moving to a new town. He had to leave all of his friends behind. So God wanted me to give the little boy a fun dream.

"In his dream, the little boy went to an

amusement park with a new friend. They rode ride after ride and laughed together. When the child awoke the next morning, he remembered his dream and said a prayer to God asking for a friend.

"Several weeks later, a family moved into his neighborhood, and of course, they had a son the little boy's age. They became best friends," Celeste said. "Now what do you think about that dream?"

"Well, that dream prompted the little boy to say a prayer to God," said Angelle.

"Exactly, God's dreams do have purposes," Celeste said. "The boy's prayer was delivered to the Wishing Well in Heaven by the prayer-mail angels.

"Prayer-mail angels, not air-mail angels, get it?" Celeste said giggling.

"Yes, I get it," Angelle said laughing.

Celeste continued, "God answered the little boy's prayer at the right time and in the right way. Isn't God awesome! I love that word awesome!"

ANJO AND MICHAEL VISIT THE KINGDOM OF LOST SOULS

Anjo's lesson taught him the importance of being himself. By accepting who he was, he would be part of the most powerful division in Heaven—God's royal army. Anjo realized that his mission and Michael's were one and the same.

"I have a place I want to show you," Michael said. "It has caused God much heartache. Grab hold."

They flew to a place of creepy darkness where shrieking cries of lost souls were constantly heard. It was an enormous area surrounded by mountains and swamps. The smell of burning sulfur was everywhere. Anjo pinched his nose closed so he wouldn't breathe the rotten, nasty odor. Then he covered his ears from the horrible cries of souls in agony.

"Where are we?" Anjo asked.

"This is Lucifer's kingdom. I want you to remember this horrid place where lost souls live for all eternity," Michael said. "This will

make you work even harder to keep Matthew on the right path of doing good."

They stood on a steep ledge of the eerie mountain. Anjo looked around. This was the worst lesson of all. The moans and groans coming from all directions caused him to swallow hard. Tears formed in his eyes.

"Michael, I will fight the bad angels with all the grace Father gives me. This is not a place for my Matthew," Anjo said with determination.

"This is not a place for any of God's children," Michael said.

"Why are all these souls here? Did their guardian angels fail them?" Anjo asked.

"No, in fact, their angels worked very hard," Michael said. "You see, Anjo, God gives to all human beings free will. This gift allows them authority over their lives. They live their lives the way they choose to. Unfortunately, these souls made many bad choices and constantly ignored their angel's guidance. It's a sad situation."

"Michael, Father can order every human being to make the right choices on Earth. Why won't He do it?" Anjo asked.

"It would not be free will if He interfered," Michael stressed. "Whatever choices people make, God allows their decisions to play out in their lives. And as you can see, these souls lost happiness with Him forever because of their poor decisions."

Anjo learned that day in the dark, dreary kingdom how much God respected every human being He created. He realized that God's plan would always be a mystery to him. Anjo knew that God knew best; he trusted Him completely.

Anjo would share all that he learned with Angelle. They had important jobs to do. This was not a place for Sarah and Matthew.

ANJO AND MICHAEL VISIT EARTH

Anjo held on tightly to Michael as they departed the Kingdom of Lost Souls.

"Where are we going now?" asked Anjo.

"I want you to see the warring angels in action."

They flew to different scenes of battles between the good and the evil angels. First, they viewed a school playground where the bad angels were encouraging a boy of twelve years old to sell drugs to two younger boys.

"The older boy wants to wear cool-looking clothes, so he makes his spending money selling drugs," Michael explained. "He's mixed up with the wrong kids."

"Well, that's not cool to me. Drugs are dangerous! Plus, he's encouraging the younger boys to make bad choices."

"Exactly! That's worth fighting for!" Michael drew his sword.

Suddenly, a sword appeared on Anjo's hip and a shield in his hand. They attacked.

Clash! Clang! Swoop! Clank! Clank!

Anjo's lesson on using weapons paid off as he and Michael joined the other warring angels on the scene. Together with the two young boys' guardian angels, they fought against the evil ones.

When the older boy heard the shouting of a teacher on duty running toward him, he ran away and the bad angels followed him. The teacher's guardian angel ran by her side. Another battle won!

What a team they were! This new experience made Anjo a believer in himself. He was no ordinary angel, but a G.A. assigned to a very important soul-saving mission.

Anjo placed his sword in the scabbard as sweat trickled down his forehead. What a magnificent feeling he had at helping defeat evil. He turned toward Michael and bowed. "I'm Anjo, Sir Michael. I'm a G.A. under God's command. Proud to be at your service."

Michael returned the bow. "Glad to have you accompany me, Sir Anjo."

They flew to other scenes of battles where three girls poked fun at another less-fortunate girl; two children cheated during a test; and four teenagers drank alcohol while riding in a car. At each scene, clashes of armor between the good and the bad angels were heard as the swords of the angels met with great force.

"All of these children exercised their free wills, ignored the guidance of their angels and made bad choices. This was very upsetting for their angels!" Michael said. "You must always remember to respect Matthew's gift of free will."

"OK, but I just wish people could see what we're seeing," Anjo said. "They would learn that good angels are everywhere, fighting battles for them. They would make better choices."

"But, that's not how it is on Earth. People have forgotten that angels are real, that God has assigned a special angel to each one of them," Michael said. "How sad it is for so many who have never learned how much God loves them."

Anjo shook his head from side to side. "That is unbelievable!"

"Anjo, Father wanted you to see the evil ones in action. You and I will always be

Angel-Brothers working together, fighting battles together against Lucifer."

Anjo had now seen the light! He thanked Michael for helping him understand how important it was to be the angel God wanted him to be. His time with Michael taught him many lessons, but this lesson would be with him forever.

TRUE BEAUTY IS ON THE INSIDE

Angelle's time with Celeste was fun, relaxing and informative. She listened attentively to every dream and story that Celeste shared and learned lessons associated with each story. Their time together flew by.

"Celeste, Father called you the Angel of Love and Beauty. How did you get your name?"

"Father gave it to me. As you can see I'm not exactly what an angel would call beautiful. Look at my blue eyes, snapple (a color in Heaven) hair and all my freckles. What a combination!" Celeste said. "I remember the day Father looked at me with His loving eyes. He told me that beauty was in the eyes of the One who gazed upon me. He made me feel like the most beautiful angel in all of Heaven." Celeste's cheeks turned a rosy pink, making her freckles fade.

"You're blushing," Angelle said.

"Father does that to me. I love Him so much," Celeste said. "Anyway, all angels look different to me. Some are tall, short, thin, chubby, pretty, not so pretty; but to Father we're all the same. Father reminds us often that what counts is the beauty on the inside, not on the outside."

"Are all people on Earth beautiful to Father, too?" Angelle asked.

"They are." Celeste stretched out in the

bed of flowers and wiggled her toes through the delicious-smelling flowers.

"Let's talk about contrast in the world," she said. "If all people were the same and there was no contrast, people would look the same and do the same things. They'd work at the same kind of jobs and earn the same amount of money. People wouldn't have to help one another because they'd all be the same."

"That makes sense to me," Angelle said.

"Earth would be a boring place to live," Celeste stressed. "If people didn't need each other, Father wouldn't need guardian angels to help guide them. Now that's an unpleasant thought for angels."

Angelle gasped and added, "And Sarah wouldn't need me."

"You got it. But, thanks to God, He made the world full of contrast where people need each other," Celeste said. "So people need guardian angels like us. We encourage them to do kind things for one another."

"What kind things?" Angelle asked.

"Some help others by giving food and clothing to the poor, visiting lonely people, caring for the sick and providing shelter for the homeless. I could go on and on. There are so many needs in the world," Celeste said. "Your challenge as a guardian angel is to help your assignment do kind things for others."

"I know now why Father calls you the Angel of Love. You teach little angels like me how important it is for people to love and help one another," Angelle said. "That will make the world a better place to live."

"You're learning very well," Celeste said. "One more thing, it's important to teach Sarah, as well as Matthew, to do things for others out of the kindness of their hearts and not expect anything in return," Celeste emphasized. "Many people on Earth expect rewards for their actions. They want others to notice what they do for others. Believe me, Father is not pleased with those people." There was no joking in Celeste's tone of voice.

"I understand, Celeste. I'll do my best to teach Sarah well." As Angelle said this, her facial expression changed. She wanted to please God in every way, but to do that meant leaving God's presence and going to Earth.

Celeste picked up on her feelings and

said, "Angelle, I know you're hurting inside because you don't want to leave Father. But you see," Celeste paused, "Father wanted you to experience how painful it is being separated from Him."

"What? Why would Father want me to hurt like this?" Angelle asked. "I feel like my heart is crushed."

With tenderness, Celeste explained, "This is one of the most important lessons for you to learn.

"This is how Father feels every time one of His children fails to return to Heaven at the end of life. They are forever separated from Him because of their bad choices. His heart is broken in two."

"Wow! I never thought about Father's heart being broken," Angelle said. Tears escaped from her eyes and slid down her cheeks.

"You and Anjo have important jobs to

do. You two will teach valuable lessons to Sarah and Matthew; they'll pass the lessons on to other children; and children's actions will influence adults," Celeste explained. "Think of it—God is using children for an important rescue mission."

Celeste reached out her hand and caressed the side of Angelle's face. "And remember, Angelle, Heaven doesn't limit Father; nothing limits Him," she said. "He'll always be with you. Just close your eyes and you'll see His face. That's a promise." Angelle gave Celeste a big-sister hug.

At that moment, Angelle's halo began to glow. Celeste grew excited and rose above the clover patch. "It's time, Angelle."

"Time for what?" Angelle asked.

"We must go back to Father."

"How do you know this?" Angelle asked.

"Oops, I almost forgot to tell you," Celeste said. "When your halo beams brightly, Father is calling you. It's kind of like a...," she paused and thought, "a text message on Earth," she added. "We must be off. Don't want to keep Him waiting. Excitement is in the air!"

Angelle now felt like a complete and content angel. Her time with Celeste taught her many lessons, but more importantly, no matter how much distance existed between her and God, He was always with her, and His face was only a thought away.

GRADUATION DAY
HAS ARRIVED

Angelle and Anjo were overjoyed to be in God's Presence again. They thanked Celeste and Michael for their time and wisdom. They promised never to forget the many lessons learned while they were with them.

Azrael, the Head Angel, instructed Angelle and Anjo to exchange the lessons they learned with each other. They faced one another, bowed their heads allowing their halos to touch. The information was transferred through the latest advanced, halo technology as if each experienced the lessons themselves. After the transmission was complete, they joined the other student angels. Graduation day was finally here.

God presided over the gathering of angels and gave Azrael, now standing next to His throne, the signal to begin the ceremony. The orchestra leader of the Angelic Symphony began to play glorious music, and bells began to ring. The student angels marched up the aisle.

The little angels could hardly contain their excitement and stood proudly before God, their halos beaming brightly. God presented each a diploma with the word PASSED stamped in gold. Graduating from angel school was a great honor in Heaven.

God then blessed them with the final Guardian Angel Blessing:

"I bless thee with the graces
That will help all of you
Protect My children on Earth.
You are now part of
My Holy Army."

After the ceremony some little angels tested their halos to see who could outshine the other, while others tried out their permanent wings by flying to the nearest stars. It was a joyous celebration!

The time every angel in Heaven had been

waiting for had finally arrived. God was ready to create the twins. Angelle and Anjo rose above God and the audience of angels; they held hands and began to spin, pulling clouds, stars and rainbows into their whirlwind of energy. They pointed toward Earth and waited for God's signal to leave.

God raised His hands upward, then downward as electrified rays burst from them. In a flash, Angelle and Anjo were off to Earth to begin their roles as the newest A.O.A.'s – Angels on Assignment. Matthew and Sarah were now tiny cells in their mother's womb.

That's how it is in Heaven. At the blink of an eye, God prepares guardian angels and creates life on Earth. From the moment life is created, until the moment life is over on Earth, God's guardian angels are on earthly duty.

The adventures continue on Earth!

Let's Talk About . . .

Please note that some of the following things may be challenging for younger children. Select those that would be appropriate.

In this section, children are encouraged to talk with a parent. Please note that guardians and teachers are also included, but not specified.

The Holy Bible is referred to in this Let's Talk About... section. If you don't have a children's Bible, one can be purchased at any Christian book store. Finding treasures buried in this great book will be challenging, educational and fun.

1   On page eight, The Valley of Peace is described as a beautiful place. In every direction Angelle and Celeste took in scenes of beauty. Close your eyes and imagine your own scene. Draw your scene, color it and place it on the refrigerator to remind all in your family that Heaven is our true home.

Treasure Hunting time! On page nine, Celeste tells Angelle about Lucifer wanting to be like God. Find this story in the:

Old Testament, the Book of **Isaiah**, Chapter 14, Verses 12-17.

2 God had a purpose for allowing Anjo to spend time with Archangel Michael. God wanted Michael to teach Anjo the importance of being himself. "You need to be the angel that God created you to be," Michael said on page fourteen. Discuss the lesson taught in this situation with a parent.

✡ Treasure Hunting time! Michael the Archangel is referred to as the mightiest of angels. Find and read this verse in the:

New Testament, the Book of **Jude**, Verse 9. (Since there is only one chapter in the Book of Jude, chapter one is not specified.)

3 In chapter five, Celeste talked about dreams. The first dream she told Angelle about, the little girl and her grandmother, was MY dream. I was about ten years old when I had those dreams.

I saw my grandmother standing in church after she died. She turned and smiled at me—we didn't talk. After having the same dream several times, I realized that my grandmother was OK and with God. I felt happiness for her. I have never forgotten those dreams.

Share some of your good dreams with a parent.

4   The Kingdom of Lost Souls is a place that no one wants to think about. Anjo was so sad to learn about this place. He said, "This is not a place for my Matthew." Talk about ways that your guardian angel helps guide you every day.

5   On page twenty-eight, Michael talks about FREE WILL—a gift from God that you can't see or touch. Every day you make many choices and use your free will. Talk about choices you have made today and decide if they were good or bad ones.

6   Close your eyes and use your imagination! Think about a situation where you were being tempted to do a bad thing. Picture your guardian angel and the good angels fighting the evil ones for you. Share your ideas with a parent.

7   On page thirty-seven, Celeste told Angelle that what counts is the beauty on the inside—not on the outside. Discuss with a parent some of your inner beauty traits. Think about the traits that are not so beautiful that you will change.

    Treasure Hunting time! Find the lesson God teaches on inner beauty in the Bible. Read the following in the:

    New Testament, the Book of **1 Peter**, Chapter 3, Verses 3-7. (Books 1 Peter and 2 Peter are two different books.)

8 On page thirty-eight, Celeste talked about contrast in the world. She said that if all people, places and things in the world were the same and there was no contrast, Earth would be a very boring place to live. Talk about the contrast within your family with a parent.

9 Angelle loved God so much that she didn't want to leave Him. She felt like her heart was crushed every time she thought of going to Earth. At the same time, God wanted her to learn how He felt every time a soul was separated from Him forever.

   Talk about being separated from a loved one forever. Discuss how that makes you feel.

10 What are some examples of kind things that you have done for others? Share them with your parent.

✦ Talk about people who like to broadcast (let others know about) what they do for others. Celeste emphasized that God was not happy with these people. Let's go on our last Treasure Hunt! Read what the Bible teaches on charity—giving to others. Look in the:

   New Testament, the Book of **Matthew,** Chapter 6, Verses 1-4.

About the Author

photo credit: Sheryl O'Meara

Arlene Hebert, born in the small town of Jean-
erette, Louisiana, was the oldest daughter and
the second child of nine children. She attended
and graduated from a small Catholic school and
left home in 1969 to attend Charity Hospital
School of Nursing in New Orleans, Louisiana.
Upon graduation in 1972, she moved to
Lafayette, Louisiana, where she worked as a
registered nurse for a Catholic hospital for
twenty-seven plus years. She also graduated
in 1987 with a B.S. in Professional Arts from
St. Joseph's College in Standish, Maine.

She is married, has two daughters, a son-in-law
and one grandson.

Arlene saw herself retiring in the field of nursing, but God had other plans for her. In 1994, as interesting things began to happen to her, she realized the new direction for her life: writing stories for children. Since writing was never a passion of hers, none of this made any sense.

In 1995, the hospital where she worked decided to close the department she managed, and soon after she was asked to begin a medical auditing program. Arlene couldn't help noticing God's hand in all this when she learned she had to write professionally. She attended educational programs to develop those necessary writing skills.

It was during this time that Arlene explored the idea of writing children's stories. She met two women, Shirley Comeaux and Nancy Burns, whom she credits with leading her down the unfamiliar path of writing for children. Today, they are joined by Joyce Michel, and together these three ladies edit her stories. To date, Arlene has six completed manuscripts; five in the Angeltale Adventure Series.

God continues to be the unseen guide in Arlene's writing career. She is slowly learning to trust Him as she sees things coming to pass without her doing.

A friend, Dr. Huey Stevens, said it best to Arlene, "One day, you need to write the real story–the story behind all the stories."

About the Illustrator

Peter Berchman DeHart grew up in Lafayette, Louisiana. He attended the Savannah College of Art and Design where he received his degree in Industrial Design and graduated as Salutatorian. He currently resides in his home town of Lafayette and works as a freelance designer, illustrator and painter.

He's also a musician and member of the band, Brass Bed, and frequently tours throughout the United States.

Other Angeltale Books

The Angeltale Adventure Series is presently composed of five stories. These angel stories can be read to younger children, while older children will delight in the stories themselves. Written in small chapters, these stories capture the imagination of six to ten year old children. While the stories are fiction, they teach many different life lessons in an accepting way.

In **Angels in Training: Twin Angel School**, God's plan to create a unique set of twins with special gifts had all of Heaven excited. Most student angels worked hard, hoping to be the chosen team for the assignment. By the end of the story, the reader learns who God selected for this important mission and why. The story portrays God as a loving Father and Teacher who is patient and kind, with a great sense of humor.

In **Angels in Training: Advanced Studies**, God is involved in the education of His chosen team of guardian angels, Angelle and Anjo. He escorts them to two important centers in Heaven, the Angelization Center and the Inspiration and Message Center, where two archangels carry out God's wishes. When formal training is over, God has other surprises for Angelle and Anjo. More adventures are on the horizon!

In **Angels in Training: Promised Adventures**, Anjo flies with Archangel Michael to the Warring

Angel Headquarters, the Kingdom of Lost Souls, and Earth where he witnesses evil at work. Through his adventures, Anjo learns how guardian angels and warring angels work together as Angel-Brothers.

Angelle accompanies Celeste, the Angel of Love and Beauty, to the Valley of Peace, a respite center for God's angels. Here she learns about dreams and how God uses them, about true beauty and why contrast in the world is so important.

When their time with Celeste and Michael is over, they return to Twin Angel School for graduation with the other student angels. The story ends with the long-anticipated event, the creation of the twins. The adventures on Earth are about to begin!

In **G.A.'s on Assignment**, Angelle and Anjo are transported to Earth and arrive in the uterus of the mother-to-be. There they witness first-hand the development of two single cells into Sarah and Matthew. Angelle's and Anjo's adventures continue in their new home for the next forty weeks and end with the births of the twins. Actual growth and development facts are woven into the story and teach children about life in a very creative and accepting way. This story promises to make its readers smile, giggle and laugh.

In **The Chosen Four,** angels are summoned to the Mission Center in Heaven where everything on Earth is monitored, including sports. The angels are briefed on God's plan to change how sports are to be played; and Angelle, Anjo and the twins are part of it. The plan is transmitted to Angelle and Anjo on Earth. They can't wait to share the exciting news with their assignments. Adventures await the four of them in Heaven! This story teaches children about participating in sports for different reasons other than winning. It also focuses on the importance of being together and having fun.